baby

Happy
First Christmas
Baby girl/boy!

Blessings,
Love,
and Peace
to you
this Christmas.

Hoping you
can feel Love,
Joy,
and Peace
this Christmas
Season.

Thank you for purchasing our product.

it's really helpful for us, it means a lot.

Please leave a review for us.

Our Products

Made in the USA
Monee, IL
25 November 2022

18480049R00015